Disney
Winnie the Pooh

Pooh's Honey Adventure

By Lisa Ann Marsoli

Illustrated by Disney Storybook Artists

DISNEY PRESS

NEW YORK

Buzz Buzz Buzz

Based on the "Winnie the Pooh" works by A.A. Milne and E.H. Shepard

First Edition
Library of Congress Cataloging-in-Publication Data on file.
ISBN 978-1-4231-3593-7

8 7 6 5 4 3 2

J689-1817-1-11236

Manufactured in the USA
For more Disney Press fun, visit www.disneybooks.com

loves honey.

Pooh

He loves the way it looks.

He loves the way it smells.

He loves the way it tastes!

goes to his .

Pooh   cupboard

He wants a sweet snack.

Every in his is empty.

honeypot   cupboard

Hum-dee-dum-doo! No honey

for !

Pooh

goes to his Thoughtful Spot.

Pooh

He thinks about how hungry he is.

He thinks about eating yummy honey.

He thinks about where to get some more!

"I'll look for honey in the honey !" says .

tree

Pooh

finds honey.

It belongs to some bees.

They do not want to share!

Buzzzzzzzzzzzz

Hum-dee-dum-doo! No honey

for *!*

keeps looking.

Pooh

His tummy rumbles louder.

thinks he sees a .

Pooh   honeypot

It is really his shadow.

Hum-dee-dum-doo! No honey for *!*

Pooh

Suddenly, everything is made of honey.

Pooh

is swimming in a sea of honey.

Then his daydream ends.

Hum-dee-dum-doo! No honey for !

Pooh

stops at .

Pooh   Eeyore's house

He looks around for honey.

"My tummy sure is rumbly,"

 says.

Pooh

"Have some of these thistles," says .

Eeyore

Pooh wants something else.

He draws a picture as a hint.

"That honey looks tasty," says . "I wish I had some."

Eeyore

Hum-dee-dum-doo! No honey for *!*

Pooh

continues on his way.

He spots a !

honeypot

There is nothing inside.

Hum-dee-dum-doo! No honey for !

Pooh

He goes to see .

There is no one at home.

Hum-dee-dum-doo! No honey

for !

Pooh

Then visits Owl.

Pooh

Hooray!

There is a big honeypot at Owl's house!

honeypot

"Sorry, ," says Owl.

"I am saving that for later."

Hum-dee-dum-doo! No honey

for !

meets .

Pooh   Piglet

"Do you know where I can find some honey?" asks.

Pooh

"Yes," replies . "Here in

Piglet

this ."

tree

tries to get some honey
for .

 gets stuck.

Rabbit comes along.

He pulls out.
Piglet

Then he puts the beehive back

in the .
tree

Hum-dee-dum-doo! No honey

for *!*
Pooh

Next, the friends walk past

a stream.

A is floating past.
honeypot

 cannot catch it.
Pooh

Hum-dee-dum-doo! No honey

for !
Pooh

"Look!" cries.

Pooh

A is flying by.

honeypot

 chases it.

Pooh

He cannot catch it.

"Honey is in such a hurry

today!" says .

Pooh

Hum-dee-dum-doo! No honey

for *!*

Pooh

spots another .

Pooh   honeypot

He dips in a paw.

Nothing comes out.

Hum-dee-dum-doo! No honey

for *!*

Pooh

tries harder to get the

honey.

It does not come out!

"Hold on," says .
Piglet

He returns with their friends.

Everyone helps Pooh

remove the honeypot .

Then gives a present.

Christopher Robin   Pooh

It is a full honeypot!

HUN

Hum-dee-dum-doo! NOW

there's honey for !

Pooh

31

That night, 's tummy and
Pooh
dreams are full of honey, too!